아빠를 얼마나 사랑하는지 아세요?

To Liz with love,
A.J.

This dual language edition published in 2003
by Magi Publications, 1 The Coda Centre,
189 Munster Road, London SW6 6AW

First published in Great Britain 1994
by Walker Books Ltd, London, SE11 5HJ

Text © 1994 Sam McBratney
Illustrations © 1994 Anita Jeram
Korean translation © 2003 Master Communications

The rights of Sam McBratney and Anita Jeram to be
identified as the author and illustrator of this work have been
asserted by them in accordance with the Copyright, Designs
and Patents Act 1988.

Printed and bound in Hong Kong

ISBN 1 85430 987 0

샘 맥브래트니
글

아니타 제람
그림

GUESS HOW MUCH I LOVE YOU

Written by
Sam McBratney

Illustrated by
Anita Jeram

TRANSLATED BY
SELINA YOON

MAGI PUBLICATIONS
LONDON

아기토끼는 잠잘 시간인데도
아빠토끼의 귀를 꼭 잡고 있어요.

Little Nutbrown Hare, who was
going to bed, held on tight to
Big Nutbrown Hare's very long ears.

아기토끼는 아빠토끼가 자기의 말을
듣고 있는지 궁금했어요.
"아빠를 얼마나 사랑하는지 아세요?"
아기토끼가 물었어요.
"글쎄, 잘 모르겠는데."
아빠토끼가 대답했어요.

He wanted to be sure that Big Nutbrown
Hare was listening.
"Guess how much I love you," he said.
"Oh, I don't think I could guess that,"
said Big Nutbrown Hare.

"이만큼이요." 아기토끼는
팔을 넓게 벌리며 말했습니다.

"This much," said Little
Nutbrown Hare, stretching out
his arms as wide as they could go.

아빠토끼의 팔은 훨씬 더 길었어요.
"아빠는 이만—큼 너를 사랑한단다."
'야, 그건 굉장하다.'
아기토끼는 생각했어요.

Big Nutbrown Hare had even
longer arms.
"But I love YOU this much," he said.
Hmm, that is a lot, thought Little
Nutbrown Hare.

"나는 아빠를
이만큼
사랑해요."
아기토끼는
팔을 높이
올리며
말했어요.

"I love you
as high as
I can reach,"
said Little
Nutbrown
Hare.

"아빠도 너를 이만-큼
높이 사랑하는걸."
아빠토끼가 말했어요.

"I love you as
high as *I* can
reach," said Big
Nutbrown
Hare.

′야, 굉장히 높다.
내 팔도 저만큼 길었
으면,′ 아기토끼는
생각했어요.

That is quite high,
thought Little
Nutbrown Hare.
I wish I had arms
like that.

그때 아기토끼는 좋은
생각이 떠올랐어요.
거꾸로 서서 나무에
기대고 발을 높이
올렸어요.

Then Little Nutbrown
Hare had a good idea.
He tumbled upside
down and reached
up the tree trunk
with his feet.

"나는 발 닿는
높이 만큼 아빠
를 사랑해요."
아기토끼가
말했어요.

"I love you all
the way up to
my toes!"
he said.

"아빠도 네 발이 올라간
만큼 널 사랑한단다."
아빠토끼는 아기토끼를
높이 들어올리며
말했습니다.

"And *I* love you all the
way up to your toes,"
said Big Nutbrown
Hare, swinging
him up over
his head.

"나는 이만-큼
아빠를 사랑해요."
아기토끼는
웃으며 높이

깡충깡충
뛰었어요.

"I love you as high
        as I can HOP!"
laughed Little
        Nutbrown Hare,

bouncing up
        and down.

"아빠도 이만-큼 너를 사랑한단다."
아빠토끼는 웃으며 귀가 나무가지에
닿을 만큼 높이 뛰었어요.

"But I love you as high as *I* can hop," smiled
Big Nutbrown Hare – and he hopped so
high that his ears touched the
branches above.

´야, 멋있다!
나도 저렇게
뛸 수 있다면.´
아기토끼는
생각했어요.

That's good
hopping,
thought Little
Nutbrown
Hare. I wish
I could hop
like that.

"나는 멀리 강까지 가는 길만큼 아빠를
사랑해요." 아기토끼는 크게 외쳤어요.

"I love you all the way down the lane as far as
the river," cried Little Nutbrown Hare.

"아빠는 강 건너 언덕 너머까지 만큼 너를
사랑한단다." 아빠토끼는 말했어요.

"I love you across the river and over
the hills," said Big Nutbrown Hare.

'야, 그건 굉장히 멀다.'
아기토끼는 생각했어요.
이젠 너무 졸려서 더이상
생각을 할 수가 없었어요.
아기토끼는 멀고 깜깜한
밤하늘을 보았어요.
하늘은 아주 멀어요.

That's very far, thought Little Nutbrown Hare.
He was almost too sleepy to think any more.
Then he looked beyond the
thorn bushes, out into the big
dark night. Nothing could be
further than the sky.

"나는 달까지 가는 길만큼
아빠를 사랑해요." 아기토끼는
눈을 감으며 말했어요.
"야, 그건 정말 멀구나."
아빠토끼가 말했어요.
"아주 아주…"

"I love you right up to
the MOON," he said,
and closed his eyes.
"Oh, that's far," said
Big Nutbrown Hare.
"That is very, very far."

아빠토끼는 아기토끼를
풀잎 침대에 눕혔어요.

Big Nutbrown Hare settled
Little Nutbrown Hare into
his bed of leaves.

아빠토끼는 몸을 숙여서
잘 자라는 뽀뽀를
해주었습니다.

He leaned over and
kissed him good
night.

그리고는 아기토끼 옆에 엎드려서
미소를 지으며 속삭였어요.
"아빠는 달까지 갔다가, **다시
돌아오는만큼** 너를 사랑한단다."

Then he lay down close by
and whispered with a smile,
"I love you right up to the moon –
AND BACK."

Guess how much I love you = Appa